The
MOLES
and the
MIREUK

The MOLES

A Korean Folktale

Houghton Mifflin Company Boston 1993

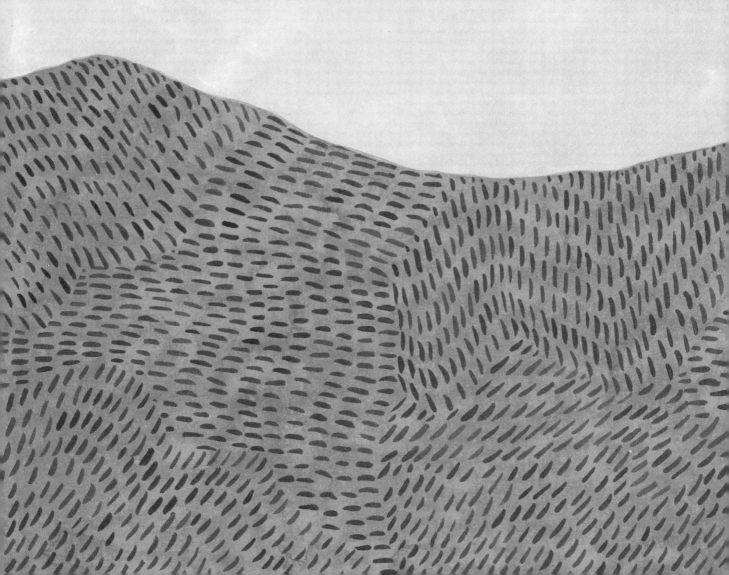

and the MIREUK

Retold by
HOLLY H. KWON

Illustrated by
WOODLEIGH HUBBARD

Library of Congress Cataloging-in-Publication Data

Kwon, Holly H.
   The moles and the mireuk : a Korean folktale / retold by Holly H.
Kwon ; illustrated by Woodleigh Hubbard.
     p.   cm.
   Summary: a mole goes to the sky, sun, clouds, and wind in search
of the most powerful husband for his daughter, only to find him
among his own kind.
   ISBN 0-395-64347-3
   [1. Folklore—Korea.]   I. Hubbard, Woodleigh, ill.   II. Title.
PZ8.1.K9876Mo   1993   92-437
398.24'52933—dc20   CIP
[E]   AC

Printed in the United States of America
HOR   10 9 8 7 6 5 4 3 2 1

To our lovely boys, Jeffrey-Ian and Andrew-David

—H.K.

To my father,
You have taught me much in the journey thus far
. . . I love you, Dad

—W.H.

In a peaceful mountain valley, beside a temple, stood a Mireuk. It was made of stone and was as tall as a three-story building.

Not far from the Mireuk, in a home under the ground, lived a mole family. The family had a daughter who had the softest gray fur and a delicately pointed nose. The mama mole and the papa mole thought she was the most perfect mole in the whole universe.

"Where can we find the best husband for our lovely daughter?" papa mole asked mama mole.

"What about the King of the Moles?" replied mama mole. "Surely he is the most suitable husband for our perfect daughter."

"But the King of the Moles is not the most powerful in the whole universe," said papa mole. "The sky looks down on the Mole King. I shall go to the sky."

So papa mole went to the sky.

"Dear Sky," he said,
"I think you are the most powerful master
in the universe, because it is you that looks
down on everything."

   "That's right," said the Sky. "I do look
down on everything, but I am not the
highest master in the universe. It is the sun
that tells me when I am to be bright or
dark! Go find the sun."

So papa mole went to the sun.

"Dear Sun," he said,
"I think you are the most powerful master in the universe, because it is you that orders the sky to be bright or dark."

"That's right," said the Sun. "In the daytime, I order the sky to be bright or dark and make the earth become warm or cold. And at night, my brother the moon and my sisters the stars light the sky. But we are not the highest masters in the universe. It is the clouds that tell us when our faces are to be seen! Go find the clouds."

So papa mole went to the King of the Clouds.

"Dear King of the Clouds,"

he said, "I think you are the most powerful master in the universe, because it is you that makes the sun, the moon, and the stars bright or dark."

"That's right," said the King of the Clouds. "Sometimes I cover the sun, the moon, and the stars. Sometimes I drop rain on the ground, and in the cold winter I drop the snow, too. But I am not the highest master in the universe. It is the wind that drives me across the sky! Go find the wind."

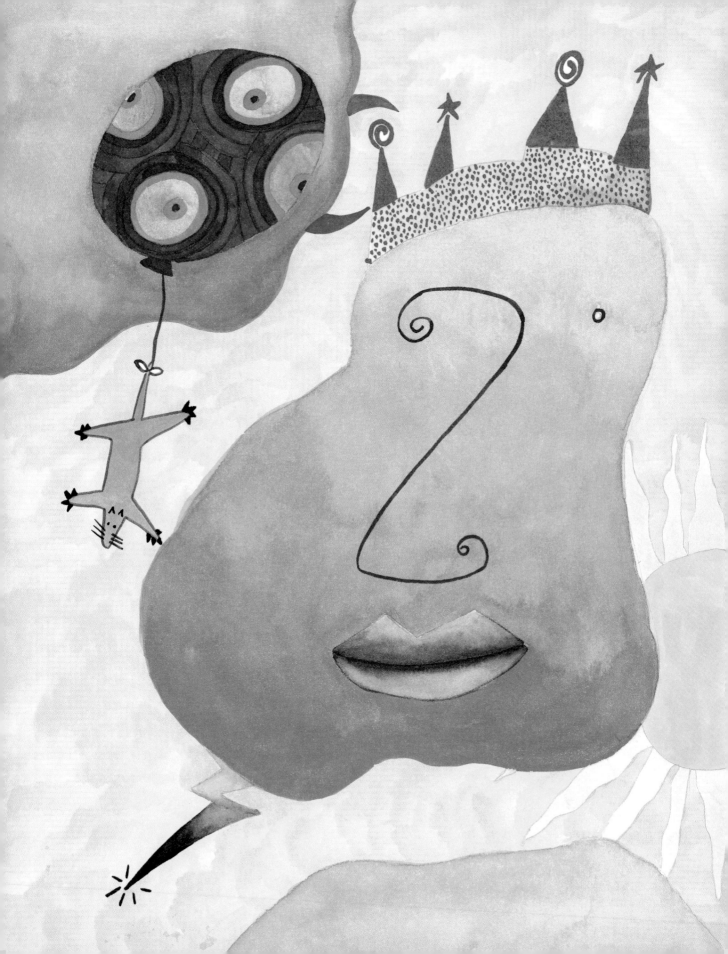

So papa mole went to the wind.

"Dear Wind," he said,
"I think you are the most powerful master
in the universe, because it is you that can
send the clouds here or there."

"That's right," said the Wind. "I can
send the clouds here or there. I like
to make sweet breezes and play with
leaves, flags, pinwheels, and kites. When
I am mad, I make hurricanes and
tornadoes that can destroy trees, houses,
cars, boats, and even airplanes. But I
cannot do anything with that Mireuk near
your home! For several hundred years I
have tried to blow it down, but still it
stands steadfast. Go to the Mireuk."

So papa mole went to the Mireuk.

"Dear friend Mireuk," he said, "the wind told me that you are the most powerful in the universe."

"That's right," said the Mireuk. "The sky looks down on me but it cannot harm me. The sun cannot melt me. The clouds, rain, and wind cannot destroy me. But there is one thing that I fear. The mole! It can dig the earth under my feet and make me topple. I have always been glad that you did not make your home beneath me."

So papa mole chose a fine young mole from
the neighborhood to marry his daughter. The
young moles were very happy, and papa mole
and mama mole felt proud to have found such
a powerful husband for their perfect daughter
so close to home.